For Megan.
Incredibly missed and not entirely gone.

A special thanks to my friend and editor, Jolie Gray.

jp

LizaDoraAuthor
LizaDoraAuthor
www.lizadora.com

ISBN: 978-0-692-59885-6

Lena Likes Lizards

Written and Illustrated
by Liza Dora

Lena loves the park. It has swings, and monkey bars, and the whole playground is surrounded by sand. It's the perfect place to play with her favorite truck.

Daddy sits down on the bench to watch Lena.

"I'm going to play, Daddy," says Lena.

"OK, Lena. Please stay where I can see you and have fun," says Daddy.

Lena walks over to a group of boys playing trucks near the swings.

"May I play with you?" asks Lena.

"No," says the boy in the blue shirt. "You are a girl, and girls play over there."

The boy hurt Lena's feelings.
Lena walks over to a group of girls
playing near the monkey bars.

"May I play with you?" asks Lena.

"Yes, but you'll have to get a different toy," says the girl.

"Trucks are for boys."

Lena walks back to the bench to sit with Daddy.

She stares down at the truck in her hands.
It really is her favorite toy.

"What's wrong, Lena?"
asks Daddy.

"The boys said I couldn't play with them because I'm a girl, and the girls said I can only play with them if I have a toy made for girls."

"Lena, things don't have to be 'just for girls' or 'just for boys'," says Daddy.

"Think about all the different things you like to do. Has being a girl ever stopped you from doing them?"

Lena thinks...

Lena
likes
lizards,
and
Lena
likes
blocks.

Lena likes exploring, and Lena likes rocks.

Lena likes elephants, turtles and mice.

Lena likes hot chocolate and skating on ice.

Lena likes football
and building with tools.

Lena likes ice cream and swimming in pools.

Lena likes dancing
and reading a book.

Lena likes stirring to help Momma cook.

Lena likes dribbling alongside her dad.

Lena likes drawing with a pen and a pad.

Lena likes robots
and playing with
cars.

Lena likes
volcanoes
and looking
at stars.

Lena likes singing and riding a bike.

Lena turns to her daddy,
"Maybe we should
just let people
do the things
that they like."

Daddy thinks that
is a great idea.

And Lena does, too.

Liza Dora is an author and illustrator living in Texas with her husband, daughter and exhaustingly lovable English bulldog, Dexter. A former teacher and coach, Liza has a B.A. in Chemistry from Texas A&M University and loves all things Aggie. She was diagnosed with an ocular melanoma in February of 2015 and published her first children's book, *Is Lena Pretty?*, in April of that same year.

Discussion Questions:

Why do you think Lena's feelings were hurt?

What were some things Lena liked to do?

What are some things you like to do? How would you feel if someone told you that you couldn't because it wasn't for girls/boys?

What was Lena's idea at the end of the book?

What would you tell someone if they said one of your favorite toys or activities wasn't for girls/boys?

CPSIA information can be obtained
at www.ICGtesting.com
Printed in the USA
LVHW07n1513020518
575703LV00016B/309/P